MURDER ON SAINT PATRICK'S DAY

A RIDGEWAY RESCUE MYSTERY

P. CREEDEN

Hear about P. Creeden's newest release, FREE books when they come available, and giveaways hosted by the author—subscribe to her newsletter:
https://www.subscribepage.com/pcreedenbooks
All subscribers also get downloadable copy of the PUPPY LOVE coloring book.

Ridgeway Rescue Mysteries can be read in 1-2 hours. Perfect for when you're waiting for an appointment or just want a fast read. Don't miss out on this quick, clean, cozy mystery that will keep you guessing until the end!

It's Saint Patrick's Day and 20-year-old Emma Wright is working hard at training five-month-old Molly, her foster puppy, to become a therapy dog. But her training coach and neighbor gets an emergency call, cutting the lesson short, and Emma volunteers to pick up her daughter at a Saint Patrick's Day concert in town.

When Emma arrives, the concert has just finished up, and the teenage girls are visiting with the band. Then the lead singer stumbles and falls to the ground, dead. Emma becomes the only level head in the crowd and calls for help. When the Sheriff and Colby arrive, they investigate it as a potential accident. But Emma finds subtle clues that something more sinister is going on. Did the leader of the band die in an accident, or was it murder?

CHAPTER ONE

E mma held the treat above Molly's nose and asked her, "Sit?"

The Saint Bernard tilted her head and continued to stand, wagging her tail behind her. Emma frowned. "Come on, Molly, work with me here."

"Not bad, Emma, but try to make it less of a question and more of a command. Therapy dogs need to be obedient and gentle. Molly has gentle down pretty well, but you're going to have to work on the obedience part if this is going to be the right career path for her," Carla Greenwood said with a smile, her eyebrow lifted as she continued to watch Emma.

Determined to do better, Emma steeled herself,

inhaled and deepened her voice to sound like her father, "Sit, Molly."

Molly blinked and lowered her haunches to the floor.

Emma nearly leaped in the air to do a fist pump, but contained herself, gave the puppy her treat and a big hug. "Good girl!"

With the first step in training Molly to become a therapy dog completed, Emma finally felt the dream she had for Molly could be a reality one day. Puppies do not normally become therapy dogs, and the AKC only recognizes them when they are one-year-old, but Mrs. Greenwood had let Emma join the class anyway. They had been neighbors while Emma was growing up, and while in high school, Emma even babysat Mrs. Greenwood's daughter, Stacy. There were four other dogs in the class, and none of them as big as Molly, even though they were full-grown. Even the Labrador Retriever next to them stood a little shorter at her full height.

Yellow painted the walls of the bright room at the community center, and the lacquered hardwood floor beneath them helped if any of the dogs were to have an accident. Molly had been running wild when they first got there, over-excited to see the other dogs. She had only just calmed down enough to give Emma a modicum of attention.

Mrs. Greenwood stood toward the front of the room, clapping her hands to gain everyone's attention. "Remember, folks, the goals we have for these dogs is that they are friendly with strangers, quiet and calm, and good with other dogs and animals. This course will help accustom the dogs to situations they may experience when they are in real-life situations as therapy dogs and help them to become attuned to their handler through respect as well as affection."

Emma smiled from ear to ear as she couldn't wait to see what the course had in store for her and Molly. She listened carefully to Mrs. Greenwood's instructions and followed them to the letter. The class continued on until the clock on the wall said it was nearly nine p.m., the ending time for the session.

"I'm so happy that you all have decided to bring your pets in for the opportunity for them to become better, happier animals socially—for them to serve their community as an active partner with you. Therapy dogs are an essential part of some patient's well-being and recovery. From offering a non-judgmental listening ear for speech therapy patients to offering warm hugs for our seniors, the therapy dog is a much-needed part of the healing process. I hope you all will join me for the next session, and we'll still take new students next week as well. Good night." Mrs. Greenwood smiled and headed over to the table where she'd put out refreshments at the start of the class.

Emma met her there. "Do you need any help packing things up?"

Mrs. Greenwood smiled and nodded. "Absolutely. Thanks for the offer."

The two of them began to pack away the remaining packets of cookies and the couple jugs of juice into milk crates, that made the supplies easier for them to carry. Sliding Molly's leash over her wrist, Emma helps her carry a box. Then as they were getting ready to head toward the exit, Mrs. Greenwood's phone rang.

She set her box back on the table to answer it, and the smile on her face disappeared, replaced by a deepening frown, her brows knitting. She blinked hard. "Okay. I'll be right—Hello?"

The blood had drained from her face as she hit the button on her phone a few times. "It's dead."

"Is everything okay?" Emma asked, setting her box down and putting her hands on Mrs. Greenwood's shoulders. "Do you need something? Maybe you should have a seat?"

She shook her head. "I... I need to go."

Emma frowned. "Go where? What's wrong?"

Mrs. Greenwood's brown eyes became focused on Emma's. "My sister's been in an accident. She... she's at the hospital now. My phone died before I could even find out what room she's in... if she's in one..."

Emma swallowed hard. "That's awful. Is she going to be okay? Do you need me to drive you to the hospital?"

She blinked. "No, I can do it. She's not hurt seriously—just broke her arm. I've told her a million times riding a motorcycle was bad for her health but she just doesn't listen."

Relief washed over Emma. "I'm so glad things aren't terrible."

"But Sarah needs me to get to the hospital to pick her up since she doesn't have a ride home. She's going to get an earful." Mrs. Greenwood forced a smile and picked up her crate once more. "It's just when she first told me she'd been in an accident, my heart sank, you know. And then I started thinking about all the different ways she could have hurt herself... and then my phone died."

"I understand completely." Emma took hold of her crate once more and followed after Mrs. Greenwood.

"Oh no!" Mrs. Greenwood stopped suddenly.

"What is it?"

"Stacy is at a Saint Patrick's Day concert at that coffee shop on Main Street. I'm supposed to pick her up as soon as class was over. I forgot when I found out I needed to go to the hospital. The hospital's in the opposite direction, and Stacy is a total germaphobe—she's not going to be happy to hear we're going to the hospital. I'm going to hear all about MRSA and other bugs that go through the hospital. Where on earth does she learn these things? I blame her father."

Emma shook her head. "Don't worry. I can pick her up. It's on the way for me."

"Really? No, I'll call one of her friend's parents... wait. I forgot my phone was dead again."

"Are you sure you're okay. You're not thinking clearly. Maybe we should call you a taxi or ride share?"

Mrs. Greenwood forced a smile. "No, seriously. Don't worry about me. But honestly, it would be a help if you could pick up Stacy at the concert. She's at the Main Street Café. But her dad's out of town and no one is at home..."

"No sweat. I have no problem getting her and taking her to your house. I'll even stay with her until you get home. She has a key, right? Do you need something else? You could take my phone with you, just in case? You're sure you're okay to drive?"

"Yes, she has a key. I'm okay. And I have a charger in the car, but with my battery completely dead it will be ten to fifteen minutes until I can get a charge enough to use it. The old thing—I really ought to get a new phone. The battery doesn't even last all day."

They reached Mrs. Greenwood's car in the parking lot, she still drove the same silver mini-van that she had when Emma was in high school. This night was just full of old memories. She assured Mrs. Greenwood once more that she would take care of Stacy, then watched as her neighbor pulled the car out of the lot, promising herself that she'd call her dad and have him follow the woman to the hospital if she even so much as forgot to use a blinker. Emma knew that when she was in an emotional state, she wasn't fit to drive. She worried that Mrs. Greenwood might not be either.

Emma knelt down and ran her hands through Molly's long, fur straight down to the warm skin underneath. "Good girl, Molly. You'll really have a blast going over to the Greenwoods' house. They have a beautiful little Pomeranian named Gracie."

Molly tilted her head and wagged her tail. Emma would swear the dog understood every word she said sometimes. She opened the back hatch of her silver SUV and asked the Saint Bernard to hop up into the back. The air outside had just the slightest chill to it, and she shivered in the breeze, hugging her green sweatshirt to herself as she headed toward the driver's side of the vehicle.

CHAPTER TWO

Main street of Ridgeway hosted several small shops and restaurants, the Capri Twin movie theater and the local library. The sheriff's office and fire station were also at the south end of the street. Emma found a parking area down an alley off to the side of the Main Street Café, and only two other cars sat in the lot.

Emma peered over at the café at the corner of the strip of shops on Main Street. The lights within illuminated the large area, and she could see that the people on stage were clearing out. The café itself was still about half-full, though more and more people were leaving via the exit.

On Valentine's, Emma and her good friend, Rachel, had visited the same café and had discovered the pet-friendly outdoor dining area. With a smile, Emma grabbed her leash and swung around to the back end of the SUV. After snapping the leash on Molly, Emma asked, "Are you ready?"

The Saint Bernard gave an excited yip before she hopped out of the vehicle, and Emma shut the hatch. Together they walked across the street to the closing café. More cars pulled out of the smaller lot directly in front of the café, and a small crowd was forming just outside the front of the door. About six teen girls giggled with excitement, and then grew to a magnified wail as the glass door to the café opened and three men about Emma's age stepped out of the building.

The one at the front had his hair dyed green and smiled wide toward the girls. His leather jacket swung over one shoulder and had as many studs on it as there were piercings around his nose and face, it seemed. Emma wondered exactly what kind of music this band played.

One of the other artists behind him had a guitar strapped to his back, and a band t-shirt with the band's logo, "Kiss me, I'm Irish" on it. With the band's name, "Irish," written in red lipstick. He waved his hands at the girls, and Emma was struck with the fact that he wore a ring on nearly every one of his fingers, even his thumb.

The third member of the band twirled drumsticks between his fingers. He was winning the contest to see who could have the most piercings in their face among the band members. Each of his eyebrows had more silver than hair.

"Hope you all enjoyed the show tonight!" the band's leader yelled above the crowd, and then he lifted his hands and began making pinching fingers. "Shall we see who forgot to wear green for our great Saint Patrick's day?"

The girls squealed and giggled, but most of them wore band t-shirts themselves, which displayed the appropriate color. Emma smiled. Some of those girls might have been disappointed.

"I know what you did!" a man yelled from off the side, stepping closer and pushing the band's leader. "She was just a baby and you took advantage of her!"

Molly growled and scooted closer to Emma's leg. Emma reached into her pocket and took her cell phone in hand, just in case she'd need to call her father.

The young man pushed the band leader again, and the band leader fell backward, toward the drummer and the guitarist. His jacket fell to the side. A manger from inside the café pushed open the glass door and helped catch the band leader before releasing him and grabbing a hold of the belligerent one. "Chris, hold on. Now's not the time for this, there are kids around."

Chris flexed his fists, his brow knit. The light from the café made his blue eyes shine brighter and glinted of his close-cropped silver-blond hair. "Now's the perfect time for this. He messed with my sister, and so help me, I'll make sure he never messes with another girl like that again!"

The band leader hadn't stood tall yet, and was hard to see through the crowd, but Emma heard him. "I... I can't breathe. Help."

"Step back everyone—give Kellum some air!" the guitarist shouted.

The crowd parted, and Kellum collapsed onto the ground, sitting cross-legged, his hands still on his chest. "I.. I can't breathe. Someone call 911."

Emma was already on it. She rushed over to the man's side and as soon as the dispatcher picked up the line, she yelled, "Connie! Tell my dad and get an ambulance over to Main Street Café right away. Someone has collapsed and is struggling to take a breath."

Chris the man who had attacked him stood over him, yelling once more. "Good! I hope you die."

Stacy stood among the girls in the crowd, her eyes wide.

Emma snapped her phone closed and approached the girl, blocking her view of the man on the ground. "Stacy. It's me, Emma."

Stacy barely pulled her gaze from the man to meet eyes with her. Then she frowned. "What's going on, Emma? Is Kellum going to be okay?"

Emma pushed Molly's leash into Stacy's hand. "My dad is on the way. Here. Hold Molly for me while I see what I can do to help, okay?

After blinking a couple times, Stacy nodded. Emma nodded back and then turned back to the band member sitting on the ground. "Kellum, right? Help is on the way. Tell me what you're feeling."

"I can't... I can't breathe." The man's face had gone pale and his eyes wide. His breaths came in short gasps.

"Were you hurt somewhere? Are you allergic to anything?"

"Peanuts." He nodded. "My back stings."

He barely kept his eyes open long enough for Emma to check them for changes in his pupils, then she went around to his backside and examined the back of his green shirt. She found a small hole in the fabric, right under his shoulder blade. Sirens wailed in the distance. Emma swallowed, and grabbed the bottom hem of Kellum's shirt. "I'm going to lift this, so I can see your back, okay."

Between short breaths, he nodded.

Emma lifted the shirt and revealed Kellum's bent over back. She examined it and she found the smallest red dot just between two ribs. Puncture wound.

The ambulance pulled up.

The guitarist stood over Kellum and glared at the café manager. "We told you to keep peanut products out of the dining area if we were going to play here. Did you do it?"

The manager put up his hands defensively. "Of course, I did."

"He's not choking," Emma said, standing and taking Molly's leash from Stacy. "I'm not sure this has anything to do with peanuts."

Colby Davidson and Emma's father, Sheriff Wright both pulled in front of the café, and began to ask the crowd to step back. Emma's heart leapt at seeing them both, but at the same time her stomach sunk. Emma pulled Stacy closer. "Your mother sent me to pick you up. Your aunt has been in a small accident and needed her."

Stacy blinked. "Aunt Sarah?"

"She's fine." Emma nodded. "Just a broken arm. Don't worry."

The teenager's eyes still remained wide and she blinked several times as though trying to understand the situation and everything that was going on.

Colby's gaze met Emma's. His brow furrowed. "You're here?"

She shrugged, offering him a shy smile in greeting. "The band came out of the café and was speaking to the crowd. The man over there with the manager's name is Chris. He started a fight with the victim and pushed him. Then the victim began complaining about not being able to breath. There's a small puncture wound just below the victim's left shoulder blade. Not much bigger than a bee sting."

Colby grabbed a pen and his pad and took a bunch of notes. Then he glanced at Stacy. "Did you witness the same? Anything to add to Emma's statement?"

Stacy blinked at him and shook her head. Tears filled her eyes. "Is Kellum going to be okay? *Irish* is my favorite band."

Paramedics put an oxygen mask on Kellum and

got him on the stretcher. Sheriff Wright came close by.

"Dad!" Emma called out. "Be sure the doctors check the puncture wound on his back. I think it has something to do with his condition. It might be a bee sting. He said he's allergic to peanuts, but maybe he's allergic to bees too."

Emma's father nodded and helped the paramedics load the man into the ambulance. Then he addressed the small crowd. "I'm going to need to question each of you about this incident before I let you leave. If we could all please collect back inside the café, and we ask that you do not discuss the details with one another. We don't want anyone to supplement their memories with what someone else says." The sheriff glanced at Emma. "Keep an eye on things in the other room while I question people out here, will you?"

Emma nodded. And kept an arm around Stacy as they filed back through the door. The manager glared the Saint Bernard puppy, but his eyes locked onto the therapy dog logo on Molly's harness and allowed her inside. The tension in Emma's shoulders unknotted, and she followed the remaining witnesses inside the café.

CHAPTER THREE

Molly sat at Emma's feet as she took a seat at a table close to the wall. She looked around at the small crowd gathered in the café. The two remaining band members sat at a both by the wall, glaring at Chris, the one who'd started the fight earlier while he sat at a table, alone. Stacy and the other five teenage girls sat at the table right next to Emma, because she wanted them close. And the manager remained standing and paced a bit in the room.

The sheriff and Colby stepped into the dining area, and the manager stopped pacing. Sheriff Wright removed his hat and smoothed down his hair and then addressed the manager. "Do you have any employees in the back who witnessed the incident?"

"If they were in the kitchen the way they were supposed to be, they shouldn't have, but I'll go check."

Emma's dad nodded. "Good."

Then he turned to the small crowd. "I know that it's getting late, so were' going to start with interviewing the children. Luckily, the parents are now present for most of you outside. If you'll come with me."

Emma raised her hand as though addressing a teacher. "Dad, I'm here for Stacy. Her mother was unable to come get her."

The sheriff nodded. "That's fine. You and Stacy stay here a moment, then, all right?"

Emma nodded and took hold of Stacy's hand and squeezed it. "Move over here and sit with me, okay?"

Stacy nodded, said goodbye to her friends, and then switched to sitting at the table with Emma. Molly stood up, tail wagging, and set her head on Stacy's lap. Even through tear-filled eyes, Stacy smiled and pat the Saint Bernard on the head. Emma smiled too. She had hoped Molly would make a good therapy dog in the future, and this was just a snapshot of what she hoped the puppy would do eventually.

The guitarist continued to play with the piercings on his face. Emma leaned in to Stacy. "Is that part of this band's image? All the piercings?"

Stacy's wide eyes landed on the two sitting over in the booth. "Yes. Kellum has forty-four piercings, sixteen on each ear and several on other body parts."

Emma blinked hard. "That's a lot."

"There's so many of them now that the band is know for doing the piercings themselves. I read it in an article once. I can't remember which band member got certified or something so he could do them for his mates." Talking about something else seemed to be helping calm Stacy down, in addition to Molly's presence.

Outside, the other girls who were in the group with Stacy were questioned and their parents stood by. The girls upset faces hardly displayed any more emotions than shock and dismay. Each parent took hold of their child's hand and had stood by while the girls recounted what had happened that evening as well. After a few minutes, the girls and their parents filed out to their cars. Colby and the sheriff had their heads together and were in deep conversation.

"Do you think he'll be all right?" Stacy asked, her hands still deeply imbedded in the puppy's fur.

"The paramedics came right away. I'm sure they are doing everything they can to save him. We don't know how serious his injury is or exactly what caused it. Hopefully he'll be fine." Emma didn't want to make any promises, knowing that things could turn for the worse, especially if the puncture wound on the victim's back was the point of entry for a small, sharp object rather than a bee-sting, like she originally hoped.

"What on earth is going on here? Where's Kellum?" a woman shouted from outside. Her blonde hair had green streaked on one side. She wore a band t-shirt and a leather jacket similar to the one Kellum had slung over his shoulder when he'd been attacked earlier.

Emma found herself immediately drawing to her feet, at the same time as the two band members.

The drummer started toward the front door of the building and yelled. "Monique!" He was stopped by the guitarist and the manager of the café, who had just returned from the back.

Monique stood outside with Emma's father and Colby, the deputy on the scene. The two of them seemed to be trying to explain the situation and calm the woman down.

The drummer's eyes were filled with tears. "She doesn't know what's going on. She just went around to get the van for us, so we could leave... when all this happened."

Emma slowly sank back down in her seat when the door opened and Monique came in, guided by Colby. Her eyes were already filled with tears, and her face contorted in anguish. The drummer and guitarist both rushed to her side and held her in their arms in a group hug.

Emma's father cleared his throat. "I'm afraid that this situation has been escalated. We've just been informed that Kellum O'henry died on his way to the hospital of a collapsed lung and tension pneumothorax. The doctor is now performing an autopsy to find out the exact cause of death."

Stacy wailed, and Emma drew her into her arms. The band mates also began to cry. The manager of the café stood to the side and began chewing his fingernails, a look of panic making his reddening eyes look both crazed and sad. And Chris, the belligerent man who had started the argument with Kellum at the front of the café, simply said, under his breath, "Good riddance."

CHAPTER FOUR

The sheriff seemed to be watching each of the people in the room's reactions to the news that he'd given, just like Emma had been. Sheriff Wright's attention became fixed upon the man sitting at the nearest table to him. Chris, the man in the buzz cut and scowl just glared back.

Pointing at him, the sheriff commanded, "Please state your name."

"Christopher Hendricks."

"I believe I heard the manager call you Chris earlier." Colby interjected.

"Yes, I go by Chris." The glare still didn't leave the man's face.

The sheriff sat in one of the chairs across the

table from Chris. "What is your relationship with the deceased."

Chris leaned forward on the table and continued to glare. "He raped my kid sister."

"That's a lie!" Monique the girl with the band members came rushing over, barely held back from slapping Chris by the drummer. "Kellum would never rape a girl."

Chris shook his head. "In the state of Virginia, defiling a minor is considered statutory rape, right Sheriff?"

The sheriff nodded.

"There you go. My sister used to wait tables at this café. Last year when this band came around on Saint Patrick's day, she hooked up with the band leader, Kellum. She was seventeen at the time." He glared once more at Monique. "He's not such a great guy, you know. He treated my sister like trash afterword. Broke her heart. She still cries about it, even to this day."

Clearing his throat, the sheriff tried to get Chris to focus once more. "Witnesses outside state that you physically shoved the victim twice."

"Yes, sir."

"That's at least assault. Did you happen to have a sharp object on you, too? Did you stab the victim?"

Chris shook his head, but the glare didn't leave his eyes. "No. I didn't."

"Then you won't mind emptying your pockets?" Colby asked from his position behind the sheriff.

The chair beneath him squeaked against the hardwood floor as Chris pushed it back and stood. He emptied the pockets of his jacket and jeans on the table in front of him. From Emma's angle she only saw keys, spare change, and a wallet placed on the table. "Are you satisfied? It's not like a carry around a knife."

Emma frowned. Kellum hadn't had a knife wound. It was a puncture wound from something smaller and round. Like an ice pick. She stood, squeezing Stacy's hand and letting go. "Stay here with Molly, okay. She'll keep you safe and you can keep her close. All right?"

Stacy nodded. Fat tears still sat the bottoms of her eyelids until she blinked and then rubbed them away. "Okay."

Emma approached her father and Colby. "I think it was the puncture wound on the band leader's back."

They both looked at her, brows furrowing. The sheriff frowned. "What do you mean?"

Colby nodded and leaned in toward the sheriff.

"Emma had told me about a puncture wound on the victim's back. She described it as a bee-sting. I told the paramedics as well."

Sheriff Wright nodded. "So the injury was to the victim's back then?"

"Kellum! 'The victim' has a name. Why don't you use it?" Monique yelled from a few feet away, her face even further contorted and twisted than it had been before. Her hair had become disheveled as well and frizzed wildly in all directions about her face.

Emma cleared her throat. "Yes, Kellum had an injury to his back. I believe it was likely the entry wound for whatever killed him."

"Until we get the autopsy results, we won't know for sure," Colby corrected.

"Right," Emma agreed with a nod. "It's just a theory for now, but a very workable one."

"Considering there was no visible blood on the victim, and an allergy wouldn't cause a collapsed lung, the theory is very workable. I agree," the sheriff said, pushing his chair back and standing as well.

"Are we done here? Can I put these things back in my pockets now?" Chris asked with a sigh and an eye roll.

The sheriff stopped him before he could gather his things again. "Please leave them on the table. In fact. I'd like to ask everyone who had contact with the victim shortly before his collapse to empty their pockets as well. Emma, who had contact with the victim from the time he left the building until he collapsed."

Emma blinked and then reimagined the scene. "After the v—Kellum left the café, he stood out front and spoke to the girls who were gathered by the doorway. Then Chris arrived and shoved him, twice. The drummer and guitarist and manager all had hands on him to catch him. Then Kellum collapsed and began to complain about being unable to breathe."

"If the workable theory is right, then one of the three who caught Kellum from behind could have stabbed him in the back with a small sharp object, correct?"

"Yes. It's unlikely that Chris is the culprit, since he was standing to the front of the victim. Unless he had a needle over a foot in length that could stab through the front and make a hole out the other side of the victim's rib cage. And that sort of weapon would be very difficult to conceal." Emma answered.

The sheriff nodded. "Again, I'll ask that you three turn out your pockets and place your belongings on this table as well. We'll see if we can't find a potential weapon among those items.

Slamming his drumming sticks on the table, the drummer shouted. "This is ridiculous! What motive would we possibly have for murdering the leader of our band. Do you not realize that we're out of a job right now? *Irish* was just getting ready to sign a record deal on Monday. It just doesn't make any sense that we'd do something like this. Besides, Kellum was our friend."

Monique gasped, then her lips drew in a tight line.

Emma turned to her. "You seem to disagree with something that the drummer just said. It would be better if you would just come out with it rather than holding back. If it would help us determine who the murderer is, it would be best for everyone."

The woman's eyes darted to both the two band members and then landed back on Emma, who stood next to the sheriff. "Jack is wrong." She swallowed and stood straighter, suddenly avoiding the drummer's eyes. "The band wasn't signing a record deal on Monday. Kellum was signing it. He was going solo."

CHAPTER FIVE

"Let me get this straight," the sheriff said after getting the two band members to calm down. "If these two knew about the solo record deal Kellum was about to sign, they'd have motive for murder."

"I didn't murder anyone!" Jack, the drummer yelled.

The guitarist shook his head, his eyes wide. "Neither did I. We started this band in high school. Kellum was our best friend. I don't believe it. He'd never do that to us."

Monique sobbed, her arms wrapped around her chest. "Will, I'm so sorry. He was supposed to tell you tonight after the concert. He said he didn't want to ruin your favorite holiday together. He said it was better if you all went out partying for a while afterward, and then he'd tell you."

Will's hands fisted, and he punched the table hard with a scream. "I can't believe this!"

The drummer, Jack, stepped back and sat down hard on the chair behind him. His eyes were wide and looking around as though he were in shock, tears brimming in them.

"Three out of four of you have a motive for murder, if they had discovered the victim's betrayal and are now denying it. But one of you didn't have the opportunity," the sheriff said, gesturing toward Chris before turning toward the manager of the café. "That leaves only you. You also had the opportunity to murder the victim. Please state your name and your relationship with him."

Everyone's eyes were fixed upon the manager who suddenly stood taller. His gaze darted around the room like a squirrel trying to decide which way to run while standing in the middle of the street. "Uh, I'm Drew Daniels. I'm the manager here at the café. I've known the band, *Irish* since the beginning, which is why they play here every Saint Patrick's Day. I often go out with the guys to party afterward. I don't think I have any motive for murder."

Jack laughed without mirth. "Yeah, right. Kellum only stole your girlfriend. Isn't that right Monique?"

Monique's face paled. "That was months ago."

Chris laughed too. "Drew's far from over you though. He still talks about you like you're coming back to him. It's true."

Sweat beaded on Drew's forehead. "That... that's not true."

Monique shook her head. "There's no way."

"Didn't you change your phone number, so he'd leave you alone?" Will, the guitarist asked.

Slowly, Monique nodded. "But he apologized to me earlier. Before the concert and asked that we could all be friends still."

"That's true!" Drew shouted, suddenly pointing toward Monique.

Emma frowned. "That could have been just an attempt to take away his motive before committing the murder. It's possible that the murder weapon was an ice pick, Dad. And you sent him to the kitchen before you began questioning. He could have disposed of the murder weapon there!"

The sheriff shot a look at Colby, who nodded in return and headed for the kitchen.

"This is ridiculous. I did no such thing. Chris, you were with me. Did you see an ice pick?" Drew pleaded with the angry man across the table who continued to glare.

"I didn't see an ice pick."

"There you go!" Drew answered and sat back with his arms crossed.

"But I wasn't really looking at you, so I can't say you didn't have one," Chris said with a shrug.

A devastated look on Drew's face shined through melting the moment of smugness he'd had just a flicker of before. He didn't say a word, but just shook his head, and his arms fell to his sides. Defeated.

Colby returned from the back. "The dishwasher in the back gave me the two ice picks they had back there, Sheriff."

Emma's dad took a look at the two picks, and Emma peered over his shoulder. "Those look a little thicker than the puncture wound I'd seen."

Colby nodded. "And the dishwasher got them out of the drawer in the kitchen. It had appeared that neither had been used today."

Drew seized upon it. "That's right! We haven't used the icepicks lately because our ice cube supplier started offering crushed ice for our iced lattes. We don't have to break the ice ourselves. I'm sure it's been weeks since either of them have been touched."

"Regardless," the sheriff said, placing the two ice picks in a plastic evidence bag. "We'll be checking these for any trace of blood, prints, or DNA, if you don't mind."

Drew paled again. "Of... of course I don't mind."

The sheriff cleared his throat. "I'm going to ask one last time that the three remaining suspects empty their pockets, if you please. We've determined that all three of you have both motive and opportunity. Now we just need to find the murder weapon."

The men nodded and placed their belongings on the table without another word. Wallets, spare change, keys, a pen, guitar string, and the usual items were placed on the table, but nothing too out of the ordinary.

Colby pointed at the ball point pen in front of the drummer. "Do you carry a pen with you at all times?"

Jack nodded. "Yes. Why?"

Colby leaned toward the sheriff. "If the weapon were a needle, wouldn't it be possible to conceal it within the ball point pen?"

The sheriff nodded. "Go check."

Colby stepped forward and pulled apart the pen. After examining the parts thoroughly, he lifted his head toward the sheriff and shook it. "Nothing."

Emma glanced over toward Stacy and Molly. She found that the teenage girl had sunk to the floor of the café and had begun to use the Saint Bernard puppy as a pillow. The clock on the wall above them said that it was almost eleven-thirty. She frowned. "Dad, I'm going to give Stacy's mom a call and let her know what's going on, okay?"

The sheriff nodded, and Emma stepped just outside the door of the café, choosing Stacy's mother on her contacts and hitting send while she walked.

A magazine sat upon the ground out front and began to flap in the wind. To keep it from flying away too far, Emma stomped upon it with her foot as the phone rang in her ear. She bent down to pick it up with the intention of placing it in the trash can as Mrs. Greenwood's answering service picked up.

She rolled the magazine between her hands instead of placing it directly in the trash can. "Hi, Mrs. Greenwood. I just wanted to let you know that Stacy and I are still at the Main Street Café. Unfortunately, there has been an incident here, but Stacy is fine. She and I were both just witnesses to the incident. I will bring her home as soon as I possibly can, or if you decide to pick her up yourself, just let me know. Sorry to have to have to leave a message, but I'm sure you're with your sister right now, and I hope she is fine. Will talk to you later."

After clicking the phone closed, she stepped toward the trash can and began to drop the magazine in when she found herself meeting eyes with the man on the cover of it. She nearly dropped the magazine but caught it to get a closer look. On the cover, Kellum stared back at her.

CHAPTER SIX

The March wind continued to blow Emma's hair about her face. She opened the magazine and found it to be a local college magazine with an article about the band. Apparently *Irish* had popularity among the college kids and often ran the circuit near campus. The magazine showed the band standing together with wide smiles on their faces and displayed their many piercings.

The article was about the band's many piercings and how they do them themselves. Next to it, a QR code stood out with a link to a video on line to see Jack the drummer get a piercing. Out of curiosity, Emma pulled out her phone and read the code with it, so she could watch the video.

Will the guitarist smiled for the camera, holding a needle between his rubber-gloved fingers. He used a pair of scissor clamps to squeeze the spot on Jack's ear where the needle will go. Then he said to Jack, "Take a deep breath and blow."

The video had to have been quite a little while ago, as Jack had only a few piercings compared to the one who sat in the café now. He took a deep breath and blew.

The needle pierced through the ear lobe quickly, so that half the needle stuck out on each side of the ear. Emma winced while she watched it. She'd never gotten even her ears pierced because her mother had never taken her before her parents were divorced, and her father was somewhat against it because his sister dealt with infections because of her piercings. Now that she was watching the needle do its job, she wasn't sure she'd ever want to have it done.

Will took a U-shaped ring and placed it on the end of the needle. As he pulled the needle through, the ring replaced the needle in the hole, and Will placed a ball on the other side. Then he looks at the camera with a big smile. "Now for the other side."

But Emma hit the stop button on the video and

sets it aside. Kellum didn't seem to be in the video, and this wasn't helping her learn more about the case. How someone could want to watch that video, she had no idea. It must have been for die-hard fans only. She wondered how many girls like Stacy would be influenced into trying to do their own piercings after watching it.

With a deep breath, she stepped back into the café. Colby stood over the table where the four suspects sat with their belongings on the table in front of them. Emma shot a glance over toward Stacy and found her still cuddled on the floor with Molly. Molly lifted her head and wagged the tip of her tail just a little bit before lowering her head again. Emma gave her the hand signal to stay, hoping that Molly would listen to it, even though she never had before.

Monique, the woman with the green streak in her hair, sat at the booth against the wall, alone with the guitar sitting beside her. She chewed her nails, but her watery eyes looked haunted, staring into space at nothing. Emma's heart broke for her a little bit. If she had a romantic relationship with the victim, she must have been devastated. Emma's gaze wandered over to Colby. The two of them didn't even have a romantic relationship, but she couldn't imagine if she were to lose the friendship that they had right now. She took a deep breath and shook her head to clear those thoughts from it.

The sheriff's phone rang, and he stepped to the side to answer it.

Emma stepped over toward Colby and handed him the magazine she found, then she leaned toward him and whispered in his ear, "There's an article in here about Kellum and the rest of the band as well."

He took it from her and nodded, looking down at the rolled-up magazine in his hand. "Thanks."

"How is the investigation going now?" she asked him.

He frowned, his eyebrows furrowed, and he stepped back twice, gesturing for Emma to follow him. "We're at an impasse right now. All four of them have motive, but only three have opportunity. Nothing in their possession seems to be a likely murder weapon, and we're not even sure what the murder weapon could possibly be."

Emma frowned with him. "Will you be moving the investigation to the sheriff's office?"

He shrugged and glanced over toward Emma's dad. "That's up to the sheriff."

She nodded and headed back over toward the table where Stacy sat on the floor beneath with Molly. Molly wagged her tail more in greeting, but this time, the puppy did not even lift her head. Stacy's arms were wrapped around the Saint Bernard's neck, her fingers buried in the white and brown fur. Molly seemed to know she was needed for emotional support and remained still. Emma pat her on the head before sitting in the chair behind the couple. "Good girl."

Emma glanced up at the clock and saw it was already five minutes past midnight.

The sheriff returned to the crowd and cleared his throat. "Preliminary results from the autopsy are in. The murder weapon is believed now to be a needle of at least two inches in length. Any of you willing to own such an item or know of one of the other suspects who might own one."

All four men sitting at the table frowned and furrowed their brows, but none of them said a word. The murder was unlikely to speak up, but if one of the others knew something, they weren't speaking up either.

Monique suddenly stood and rushed toward the table with the suspects. Colby darted forward and caught her by the waist, but she still managed to slam her hands on the table. "Murderer! You did this didn't you? You just couldn't stand that Kellum was going to be a success without you!"

CHAPTER SEVEN

Emma hopped to her feet, and Molly growl-whined in response. Stacy woke, her red rimmed eyes puffy and looking around as though she was uncertain of where she was. Emma set a hand on her shoulder. "It's okay, Stacy, I'm right here."

Stacy looked up at her with her bottom lip quivering. Emma leaned down and hugged her shoulders, patting her on the back. "You're okay. I'm right here. We'll be going home shortly. I promise."

Nodding into Emma's shoulder, Stacy sniffled, then leaned back and swiped at her eyes. "I'm okay. Thank you for being here with me, Miss Emma."

Emma smiled at the moniker. She hadn't been called that by anyone in about four years, but it was always how Stacy had referred to her when she was younger.

"Murderer!" Monique yelled again, as Colby pulled her from the table of suspects.

"Who are you referring to, young lady and why would you accuse the person?" the sheriff asked, placing himself between her and the table, and drawing her gaze.

"Will... or Jack. It doesn't matter. One of them did it. They are always doing each other's piercings. They have access to needles. One of them—or maybe even both of them—found out Kellum was leaving the band. They killed him!"

"That might be so, young lady," Emma's father said and held his hands out in front of him. "But we don't have enough evidence to prove it yet, so you're going to have to calm down."

Emma sat back down in her chair, and Stacy sat in the chair across from her at the table. Emma looked back over toward her. "Didn't you say that one of them was certified or something for piercing?"

She nodded. "It's Jack. I remember now."

Emma nodded. "The drummer? I just saw a video of how the piercings are done, but it was Will who did it."

"I think I saw he was apprenticing, too."

The needles used for piercing were definitely at least two inches long and from what Emma had seen, they were hollow, so they would be easier to push through flesh than an ice pick that would have a handle. But it would still be difficult to push through skin with bare hands.

Emma began chewing on her bottom lip while she looked over toward the table of items the suspects had in front of them. Was there something that could be used there like a handle or an item that would help the murder push the needle into the victim's back? For all that she could see, there was nothing simple on the table that would be easily hidden quickly in that public situation once the victim fell to the ground.

Emma frowned.

Her grandmother used to do a lot of sewing and crocheting when she was younger and had taught her to do cross-stitching. She remembered how her thumb would hurt if she pushed a needle through the fabric that had resistance. Unless she was wearing a thimble.

The items on the table were nothing that could be used in that sort of way. Not to mention there had to be a way to pull the needle back out. What could possibly be used in that sort of way?

Emma squeezed Stacy's hand from across the table and stood up. "I'll be right back."

Stacy nodded.

After drawing closer to the table and her father, she peered over the table once more to see the items there. Wallets, spare change... guitar string. Will had his hands set upon the table, each of his rings shining in the light of the café dining area. And suddenly, a possible scenario came to her.

"Dad!" She grabbed her father's arm and pulled him slightly back. "Have you checked the guitar?"

He blinked at her. "The what?"

She swallowed and pointed toward the instrument in the booth. "The guitar. Monique was right. The band members do their own piercings and are familiar with needles. I showed Colby a magazine article on it, and there's a video I watched, too."

Colby stepped over with the magazine and handed the rolled-up magazine toward her father. The sheriff glanced at the article in question. And then looked toward Colby. "Search the guitar."

He nodded and headed toward the booth.

The guitarist suddenly leapt to his feet. "What

are you doing? You don't mess with another man's instrument, man."

The sheriff slammed a hand down on the table and drew the attention back to him. "You might want to sit down, young man."

He sat down, but his eyes still never left the guitar. "I didn't give permission for my guitar to be touched. I want to make sure I say that right now."

"Exigent circumstances, young man. This is a murder investigation. If the murder weapon is hidden in your guitar, we cannot allow you time to destroy evidence."

He half-laughed. "What evidence. What on earth could you possibly expect to find in there?"

Emma spoke up. "A guitar string woven through a piercing needle, in a perfect circle to fit over your finger."

Will shot his gaze at Emma, and his eyes grew wider. He sucked in his breath.

"You had the string around your finger, half hidden under one of your rings. You used the ring to press the needle into Kellum's back, and then pulled it back out again with the string."

His mouth opened and closed like he was gasping for air.

The drummer, Jack, jumped up quickly. "Really, man? You did this? How could you?"

Colby came back with the guitar, and a needle with a string tied around it, just as Emma had described. He dropped it into an evidence bag and set it on the table in front of the suspects.

Monique rushed forward again, avoiding Colby trying to catch her this time. She beat on Will's back and shoulders. "You killed him. Murderer. How could you? All because he was breaking up the band? How selfish could you be?"

Will suddenly shot to his feet and turned toward her.

Emma's dad placed a hand on his gun. And Colby darted around the table, laying a hand on the guitarist's shoulder.

"Selfish?" Will yelled suddenly. "Me? Kellum was going to take my songs and my music with him. He had wanted look like the songwriter for the band's image, so I let him because the success of *Irish* was all of our success. But when he got this solo deal, it was because of the songs *I* wrote! Kellum was a liar and a thief. He stole you from Drew, Chris's sister's innocence, my songs from me and the band from both me and Jack. I couldn't let him get away with it."

Colby grabbed his cuffs and put them on the man, starting to tell him his Miranda rights.

The adrenaline that had been pumping through Emma's veins drained, and her shoulders ached as they fell. Sheriff Wright stepped up to her and hugged her shoulders and gave her a kiss on the cheek. "Good work, Emma."

CHAPTER EIGHT

I n the living room of the Greenwood's house, a
light sat on, but the house still looked empty.
Emma yawned as she pulled into the driveway. She
took a deep breath and looked over toward the
passenger seat, where Stacy had fallen asleep again.
It was nearly one a.m. but at least it wasn't a school
night.

Molly had been quiet in the back of the SUV.
The Saint Bernard puppy must have been tired too.
She'd been full of energy during the therapy dog
training session, barely listening to Emma's
commands, but she'd been an angel about taking
care of Stacy during the incident at the café. Maybe
she'd make a great therapy dog yet.

A yawned pulled at Emma's lips again. But she steeled herself as she knew she'd have to keep her promise and stay until Mrs. Greenwood got home. She reached over and shook Stacy gently by the shoulder. "Time to wake up, Stacy. You're home."

Stacy's eyes blinked again several times, and Emma felt sad that the pour girl had to go through such a stressful time and lose an artist that she'd admired as well. Emma knew what it was like to have a crush on a celebrity. Her crush on Colby was just as unrequited.

Lights shined behind them and pulled into the driveway next to them. Mrs. Greenwood stepped out of her car before the pair of younger women got out of the SUV. Stacy pulled open the passenger door and hopped out. "Mom!"

She fell into her mother's arms and sobbed against her mother's shoulder. Stacy's whole body shook a bit.

Emma came around the car to the pair and met eyes with Stacy's mother. The question in her eyes told Emma that she hadn't gotten the message that she'd left on Stacy's mother's phone. Emma took a deep breath and began to tell Mrs. Greenwood what had happened and why they were home so late.

The End

Look for more of Emma and Molly's adventures:
http://amazon.com/author/pcreeden

IT'S NEW YEAR'S EVE AND 20-YEAR-OLD EMMA WRIGHT HAS A DATE WITH HER crush—well, not a real date, but she can dream! Colby Davidson, the K9 search and rescue deputy, is allowing her to accompany him while he's on patrol at the Ridgeway Illumination Festival. Though they are just friends, she's still hoping for a possible kiss at the end of the festivities.

When a stranger asks them to help take some pictures at the event, Emma and Colby are happy to oblige. But their assistance turns them into alibis for the man's whereabouts while his girlfriend was killed. Most of the clues point to a robbery gone bad, but Emma doesn't believe all of them point that way. Was it really a robbery or was it murder?

It's Valentine's Day and 20-year-old Emma Wright just wants her crush to take notice of her. But Colby Davidson, the K9 search and rescue deputy only thinks of her as a kid sister. How will she get him to take her seriously?

When her veterinarian boss calls her to pick up a cat at a potential crime scene, she finds herself at the house of the richest woman in Ridgeway. Her father—the sheriff—and Colby are there. They both dismiss the untimely death as a heart attack, but Emma finds clues that it might be something more. Did the software billionaire die of natural causes, or was it murder?

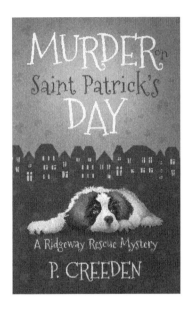

It's St. Patrick's Day and 20-year-old Emma Wright is working hard at training five-month-old Molly, her foster puppy, to become a therapy dog. But her training coach and neighbor gets an emergency call, cutting the lesson short, and Emma volunteers to pick up her daughter at a St. Patrick's Day concert in town.

When Emma arrives, the concert has just finished up, and the teenage girls are visiting with the band. Then the lead singer stumbles and falls to the ground, dead. Emma becomes the only level head in the crowd and calls for help. When the Sheriff and Colby arrive, they investigate it as a potential acci-

MURDER ON SAINT PATRICK'S DAY

dent. But Emma finds subtle clues that something more sinister is going on. Did the leader of the band die in an accident, or was it murder?

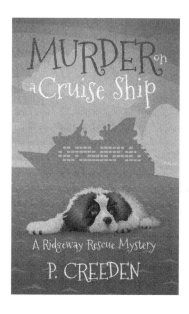

All hands on deck! It's a beautiful spring day and 20-year-old Emma Wright is meeting her crush, Colby Davidson, for a two-hour tour specifically for dogs and their owners – *The Canine Cruise*. She and Molly, the Saint Bernard, are so excited to see both Colby and Gabby, his K9 partner, as the two have been away on training.

It's smooth sailing until someone shouts "man overboard!" A news reporter who is covering the day cruise for a local station falls into the fast-flowing Potomac River, and she doesn't know how to swim. Did the reporter fall overboard in an accident, or was it murder?

Coming in May: Emma and Molly attend a wedding... where a murder overcomes the romance of the occasion!

ABOUT THE AUTHOR

If you enjoyed this story, look forward to more books
by P. Creeden.
In 2019, she plans to release more than six
new books!
Hear about her newest release, FREE books when
they come available, and giveaways hosted by the
author—subscribe to her newsletter:
https://www.subscribepage.com/pcreedenbooks
All subscribers also get downloadable copy of
my PUPPY LOVE coloring book.

If you enjoyed this book and want to help the
author, consider leaving a review at your favorite
book seller – or tell someone about it on social
media. Authors live by word of mouth!

Made in the USA
Middletown, DE
24 October 2020

22660790R00035